Katie Morag
Delivers the Mail

To all small places

KATIE MORAG DELIVERS THE MAIL
A RED FOX BOOK 978 1 782 95366 1

First published in Great Britain by The Bodley Head,
an imprint of Random House Children's Publishers UK
A Random House Group Company

The Bodley Head edition published 1994
Red Fox edition published 1997
Red Fox edition re-issued 2010
This Red Fox colour reader edition published 2014

1 3 5 7 9 10 8 6 4 2

Red Fox Books are published by Random House Children's Publishers UK,
61–63 Uxbridge Road, London W5 5SA

www.**randomhousechildrens**.co.uk
www.**randomhouse**.co.uk

Addresses for companies within The Random House Group Limited can be found at:
www.randomhouse.co.uk/offices.htm

THE RANDOM HOUSE GROUP Limited Reg. No. 954009

A CIP catalogue record for this book is available from the British Library.

Printed in China

The Random House Group Limited supports the Forest Stewardship Council®
(FSC®), the leading international forest-certification organisation. Our books carrying
the FSC label are printed on FSC®-certified paper. FSC is the only forest-certification
scheme supported by the leading environmental organisations, including Greenpeace.
Our paper procurement policy can be found at www.randomhouse.co.uk/environment

Katie Morag
Delivers the Mail

Mairi Hedderwick

RED FOX

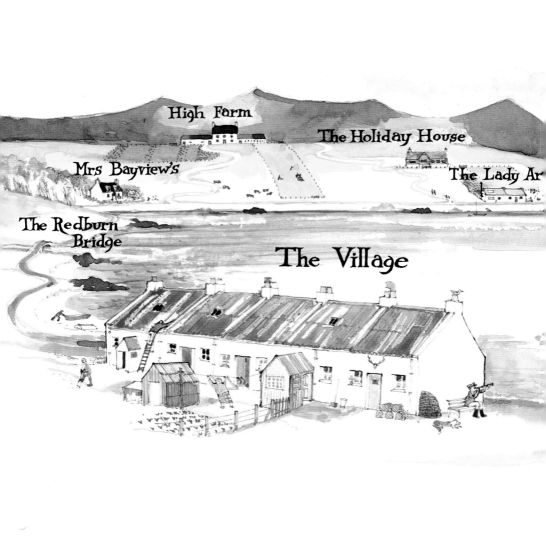

High Farm

The Holiday House

Mrs Bayview's

The Lady Ar

The Redburn
Bridge

The Village

THE ISLE of STRUAY

Grannie's

The Mainland

The Jetty

ISLE of STRUAY
SHOP & POST OFFICE

OBAN TIMES
GET YOUR COPY HERE

The Shop & Post Office

STRUAY LASS

Wednesdays were always hectic on
the Isle of Struay, for that was the
day that the boat brought mail and
provisions from the Mainland.

One particular Wednesday was worse than usual, since baby Liam was cutting his first tooth and both Mr and Mrs McColl were in a bad mood.

"All right, all right," said Mrs McColl in exasperation. "I'll take Liam upstairs to quieten him down! Katie Morag, you take the mail to the houses across the Bay.

There are five parcels – one for each house. The one with the red label is for Grannie."

Pleased to escape, Katie Morag set off. She loved any excuse to visit her grannie, who lived all alone in the very last house on the other side of the Bay.

But it was a hot day, and Katie
Morag had just stopped for a
moment to paddle in a pool beneath
the Redburn Bridge, when suddenly
– *splash!* – she slipped on a slithery
stone and fell into the water,
mailbag and all.

"Oh, dear! Oh, dear!" wailed Katie Morag, looking at the five soggy parcels. "All the addresses are smudged and I won't know which parcel is for which house now!"

Only Grannie's parcel was still recognisable by its red label.

Then, because she was so
frightened and ashamed, Katie
Morag did a silly thing. She ran
the rest of the way to the other
side of the Bay and threw a

parcel – any parcel, except the
red-labelled one – on to the doorstep
of each of the first four houses.
Nobody saw her. Still sobbing,
she ran on to Grannie's.

"Well, this is a fine *boorach* you've got yourself into, Katie Morag," said Grannie, when Katie Morag had explained what she had done.

"Still at least you've given *me* the right parcel – it's got the spare part

for the tractor that I've been waiting
for. I'll go and get the old grey lady
going, while you dry yourself up.
Then you can try and sort the whole
muddle out."

Grannie had her head under the
bonnet of the tractor for a long time.
Occasionally, Katie Morag heard

muffled words of anger and she
thought of the angry words waiting
for her at home . . .

   Then, suddenly, with a cough of
black smoke, the tractor stuttered
into life and they set off to go round
each of the four houses in turn.

The first house belonged to the
Lady Artist. She had been expecting
tiny, thin brushes for her miniature
paintings, but the parcel Katie
Morag had left on her doorstep
contained two enormous brushes.

"They're bigger than my painting
boards!" she said in disgust.

The second house was rented
by the Holiday People. They had
ordered fishing hooks from a sports
catalogue, but their parcel had been
full of garden seeds.

"We can't catch fish with daisies
and lettuces!" they complained.

At the third house, Mr MacMaster was standing by a big barrel of whitewash, holding the Lady Artist's paintbrushes.

"How can I paint my walls with these fiddling little things?" he asked.

In the fourth house lived Mrs Bayview. "That stupid shop on the Mainland! Where are my seeds? Flowers won't grow out of *these*," she said crossly, waving a packet of fishing hooks in the air.

After much trundling back
and forth, Katie Morag finally
managed to collect and deliver
all the right things to all the
right people.

Everyone smiled and waved and
said, "Thank you very much."

By now it was getting dark.
Katie Morag thought of the long
journey home. She would be
very late and her parents were
so bad-tempered these days on
account of Liam's noisy teething.

"Grannie, would you like to come back for tea?" she asked.

Katie Morag half hid behind
Grannie as they walked in the
kitchen door but, to her surprise,
everyone was smiling. Liam had cut
his tooth at last and all was calm.

"Thank you for helping out today, Katie Morag," said Mrs McColl. "Isn't she good, Grannie?"

"Och aye," said Grannie with a smile as she looked at Katie Morag. "She's very good at sorting things out, is our Katie Morag." And she said no more.